This is an Oggly

With their hearing horns, they can hear ants cough and earthworms burp.

Ogglies sleep when they feel like it, day or night.

Oggly hair is so hard that it can't be cut, even with the sharpest scissors.

Their lumpy noses adore the smelliest stenches.

Oggly teeth can crack anything: glass, iron, plastic, wood, and stone.

Oggly muscles are very strong and as tough as steel.

Oggly stomachs can digest anything. Ogglies never get tummy ache.

They like to bathe in mud and muck.

An Imprint of Starfish Bay Publishing Pty Ltd
www.starfishbaypublishing.com

THE OGGLIES GO TO SCHOOL

First North American edition Published by Starfish Bay Children's Books in 2016
ISBN: 978-1-76036-023-8
DIE OLCHIS - So schön ist es im Kindergarten © Verlag Friedrich Oetinger, Hamburg 2007
Published by agreement with Verlag Friedrich Oetinger
Translated by David-Henry Wilson
Printed and bound in China by Beijing Zhongke Printing Co., Ltd
Building 101, Songzhuang Industry Zone, Beijing 101118

Erhard Dietl, born 1953 in Regensburg, studied at the Academy of Graphic Arts and the Academy of Fine Arts in Munich. He is an author, illustrator, and songwriter. He has written over 100 books, available in translation in numerous languages around the world. Erhard Dietl has been awarded the Austrian Youth Literature Prize, and other notable literary awards.

Also by Erhard Dietl

Erhard Dietl

The Ogglies
Go to School

STARFISH BAY
CHILDREN'S BOOKS

The Ogglies live in a stinky cave at the trash dump in Smelliville. The family consists of: Oggly-Mom and Oggly-Dad, Oggly-Grandma and Oggly-Grandpa, the two Oggly children, and Oggly-Baby.
The Oggly children are playing mudball-throwing.
Suddenly a thick splodge of mud hits Oggly-Dad right on his lumpy nose.

"Turds of toads!" he growls. "You can't get any peace and quiet around here. This isn't school, you know!"

"What's school?" asks one of the Oggly children.

Oggly-Grandma is surprised. "Don't you know what school is?" she asks. "There's one in Smelliville, with lots of children. They sing songs and have recess when they eat things."

"Oggly-poggly!" shout the Oggly children. "We want to go there! And we want to go there NOW!"

Oggly-Mom hasn't got time to take them. She has to look after Oggly-Baby. But Oggly-Grandma agrees to take them. She quickly packs a couple of yummy rusty old cans for recess, and then they're away.

With a roar and a rattle, Firebottom, the Ogglies' pet dragon, takes off, and the Oggly children and Oggly-Grandma soar up above the trash dump.

Soon, they're flying over grassy green fields on their way to Smelliville.
"There's the school!" cries Oggly-Grandma.
"Just behind that building!"
They land, and Firebottom waits behind the house.

The schoolchildren are just having their break, and the teacher, Mrs. Lucy, is pouring out some hot chocolate.

"Hello! We've come to join your school!" shout the Oggly children. They take their rusty cans out of Oggly-Grandma's trash bag and crack and crunch them in their teeth.

Mrs. Lucy is about to say something, but her phone rings.

"Oh no, oh dear!" she cries into the receiver. Back at her home, the washing machine hose has burst, and now her whole apartment is under water.

"I've got to go home at once!" she cries in a panic. "But I can't leave the children on their own!"

"Relax," says Oggly-Grandma. "You just go. I'll look after them while you're gone."

"Oh, thank you very much. That's really nice of you. I'll be as quick as I can," says Mrs. Lucy, and rushes away.

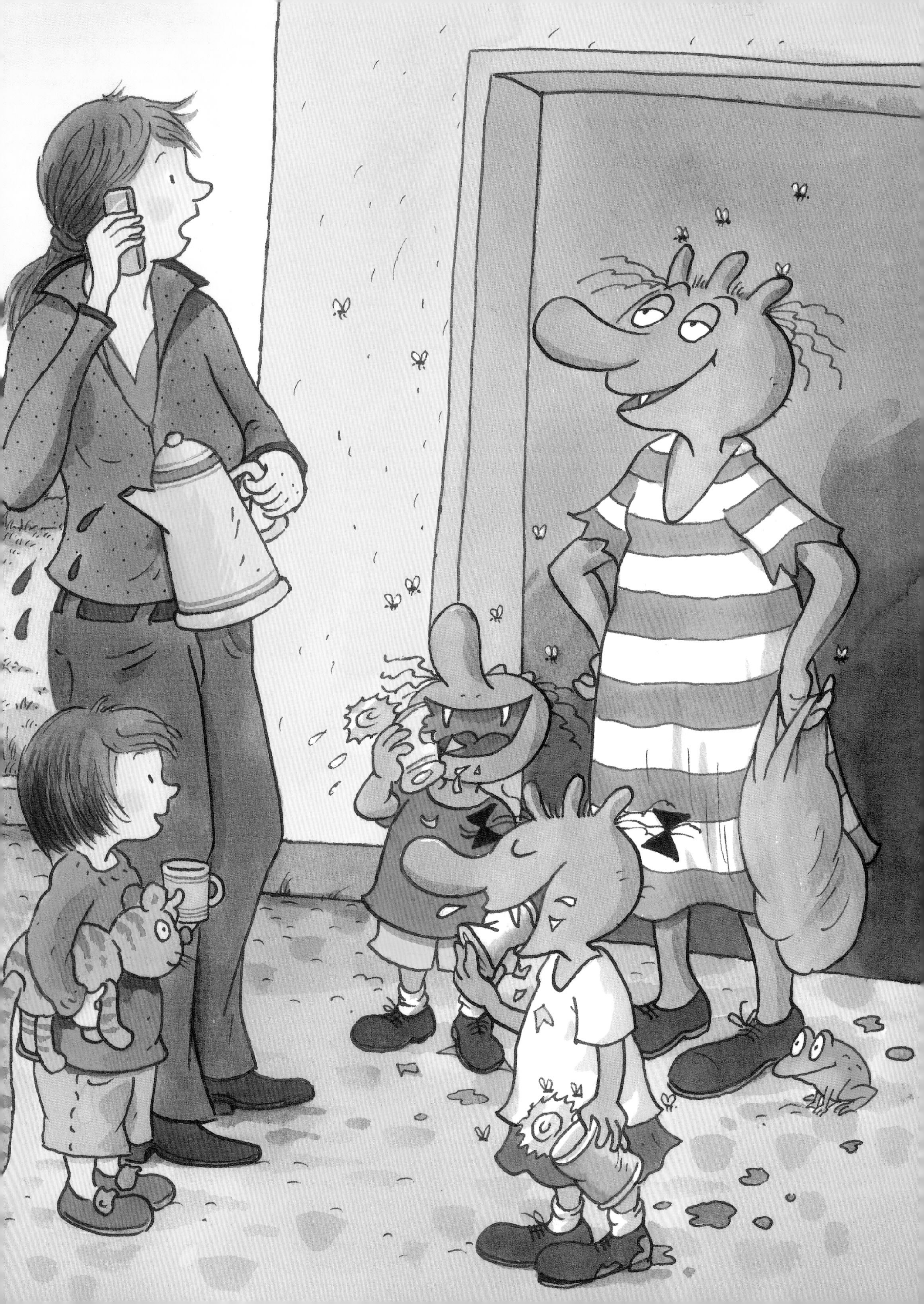

"Ok," says Oggly-Grandma to the children. "I'm in charge now, and the first thing you're going to do is draw some oggly pictures. Each of you can draw whatever you like best."

The children fetch some paper and colored pencils, and they draw lots of beautiful things: a dog, spaghetti with tomato sauce, Santa Claus, and an Easter bunny poking its tongue out at Santa Claus.

The Oggly children prefer to draw much ogglier pictures: fish bones, mudballs, hundreds of little black flies, and a toad poking its tongue out at the flies.

"Fishy fly bones, haven't you done well!" says Oggly-Grandma to all the children. "Ok, now I want to see how strong you all are. Let's go outside and do some weightlifting."

The children show her what they can
do, lifting all kinds of things: a chair, a
wooden box, a stone, and even a big red
wheelbarrow.
What about the Oggly children? They
grab Dragon Firebottom by his feet and
lift him high in the air. He's as heavy as a
tractor, but they've got muscles as hard as
steel.

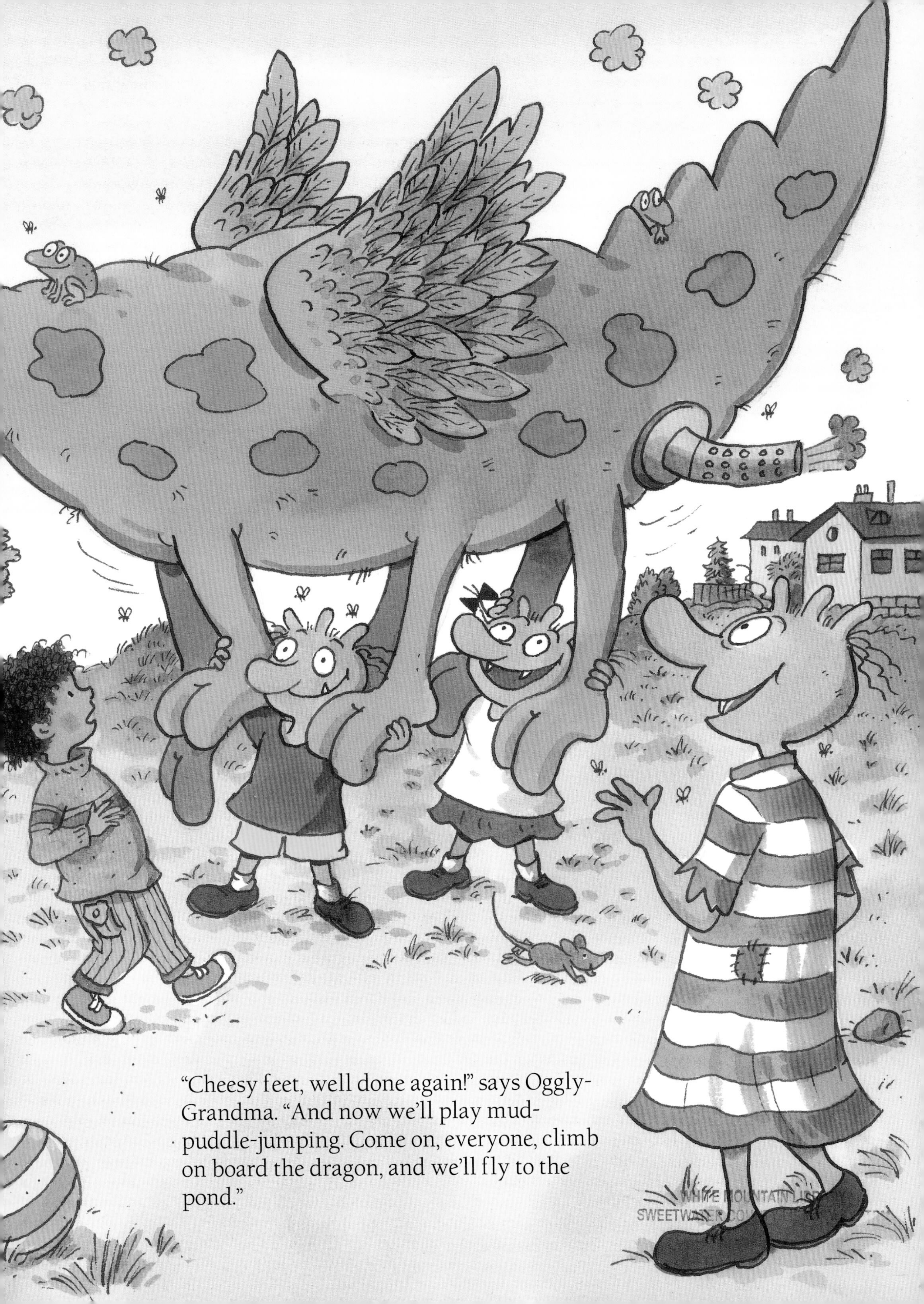

"Cheesy feet, well done again!" says Oggly-Grandma. "And now we'll play mud-puddle-jumping. Come on, everyone, climb on board the dragon, and we'll fly to the pond."

Around the pond, the ground is wet and really muddy. "Whoever splashes the farthest is the winner!" announces Oggly-Grandma and jumps straight into a puddle to send the mud spraying.
Soon, all the children are happily splish-splash-sploshing in the mud. Of course, the Oggly children do it best. They leap up high and then come crashing down on their bottoms in the mud.

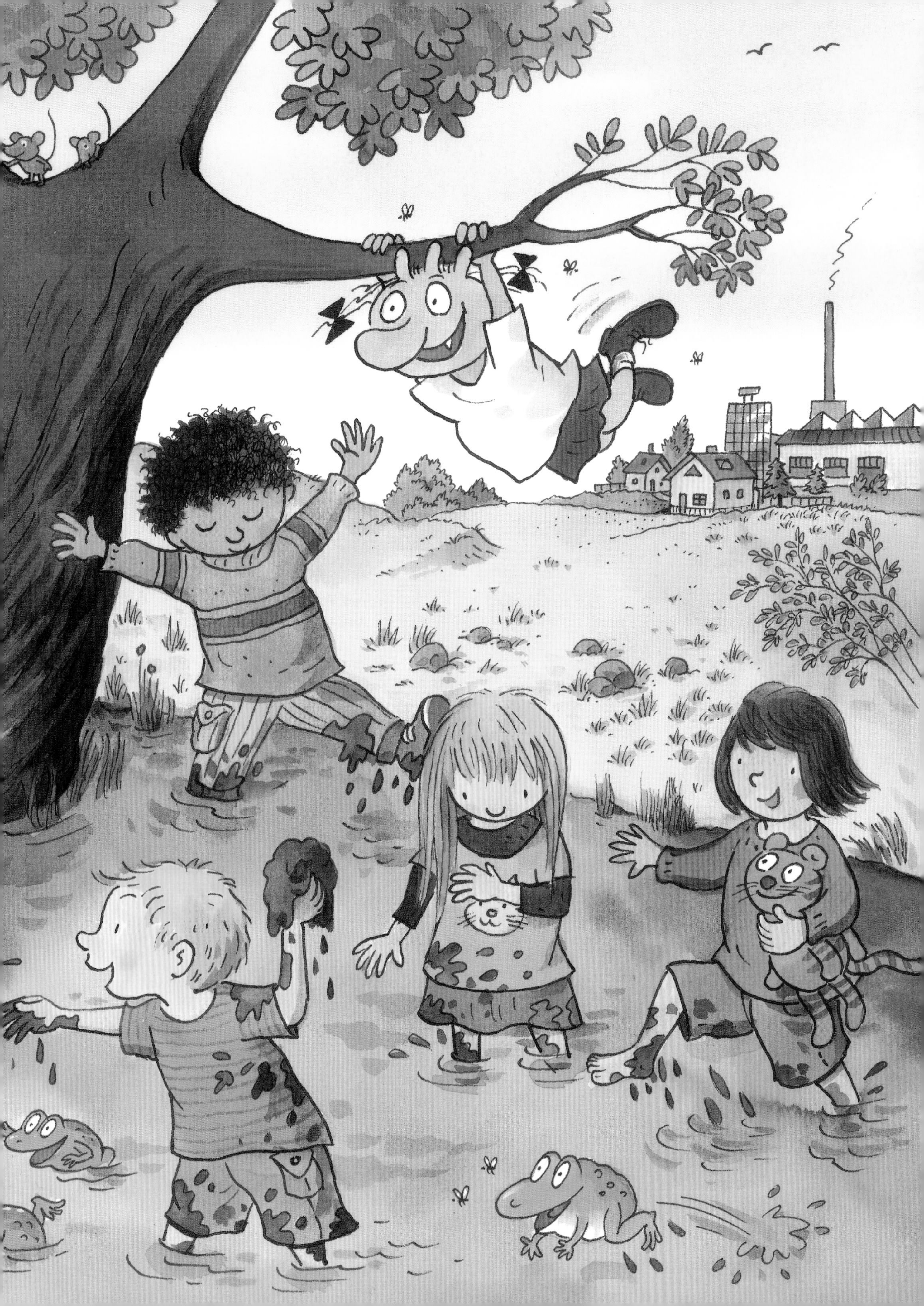

"Slimy sludge and slither slop, that was ogglorious!" cries Oggly-Grandma.
"And since we're all so nice and dirty, we're now going to sing the mudpuddle song."

We're gonna have a puddly party,
Gonna make it fine and farty,
Gonna make ourselves all yucky,
Noone's ever been so mucky.

Hee hee hee, when flies pee,
There's not much that you can see.
When we do oggly poo,
There's enough to fill a zoo.

We're gonna have a puddly party,
Gonna make it fine and farty,
Gonna make ourselves all yucky,
Noone's ever been so mucky.

Squish and squelch, grease and grime,
Ogglies love the slurpy slime.
Mud and muck, dirt and dung —
Now our puddly song is sung.
Mud and muck, dirt and dung -
Now our puddly song is sung.

"Toads and tadpoles!" cries Oggly-Grandma, "you sang that beautifoggly!"
Little Louisa puts her hand up. Her sludgy hair is hanging over her face like brown spaghetti.
"I don't think Mrs. Lucy will like it if we're all so dirty. When she comes back, she'll be angry."
"You're right," says Oggly-Grandma. "Unfortunately, Mrs. Lucy is not an Oggly."
She has a little think, and then she smiles. "Firebottom can help us."

The dragon stands beside the pond, sucks up some water, and then blows a powerful jet over Louisa, just like a garden hose. Louisa is now soaking wet, but as clean as a flower in a shower.

The other children follow in turn: Patrick and Nina, Tom, Ali, and Eva. Only Lena doesn't want to go, because she really likes her new mud brown hair. But she has to go anyway. Everybody has to be washed and watered — even the Ogglies.

"Well done, Firebottom!" says Oggly-Grandma. "But now we need to get dry."

Like a giant hairdryer, the dragon blows warm air out of his mouth. The children stand in a row, and he blow-dries them all in turn.

Then Oggly-Grandma announces, "Now we shall all fly back to the school, and I shall tell you a nice oggly story."

Back at the school, the children sit on their chairs, and now they're all ears.
"Listen carefully, you dear little stinky-feet," says Grandma-Oggly "Once
upon a time, there was a little Oggly and a great, big, nasty white shark.
One day, the little Oggly was happily sailing over the sea when..."
At this moment, Oggly-Grandma is interrupted. The door opens, and in
comes Mrs. Lucy.
"Hello," she says, "I'm back. Is everything all right?"
"Everything's oggly-poggly," answers Oggly-Grandma. "No problem."

"Thank you for helping me," says Mrs. Lucy. "And of course the two children are welcome to come back tomorrow. But now it's time for everyone to go home."
"What about the shark and the Oggly?" cry the children.
"I'll finish the story another time," promises Oggly-Grandma.

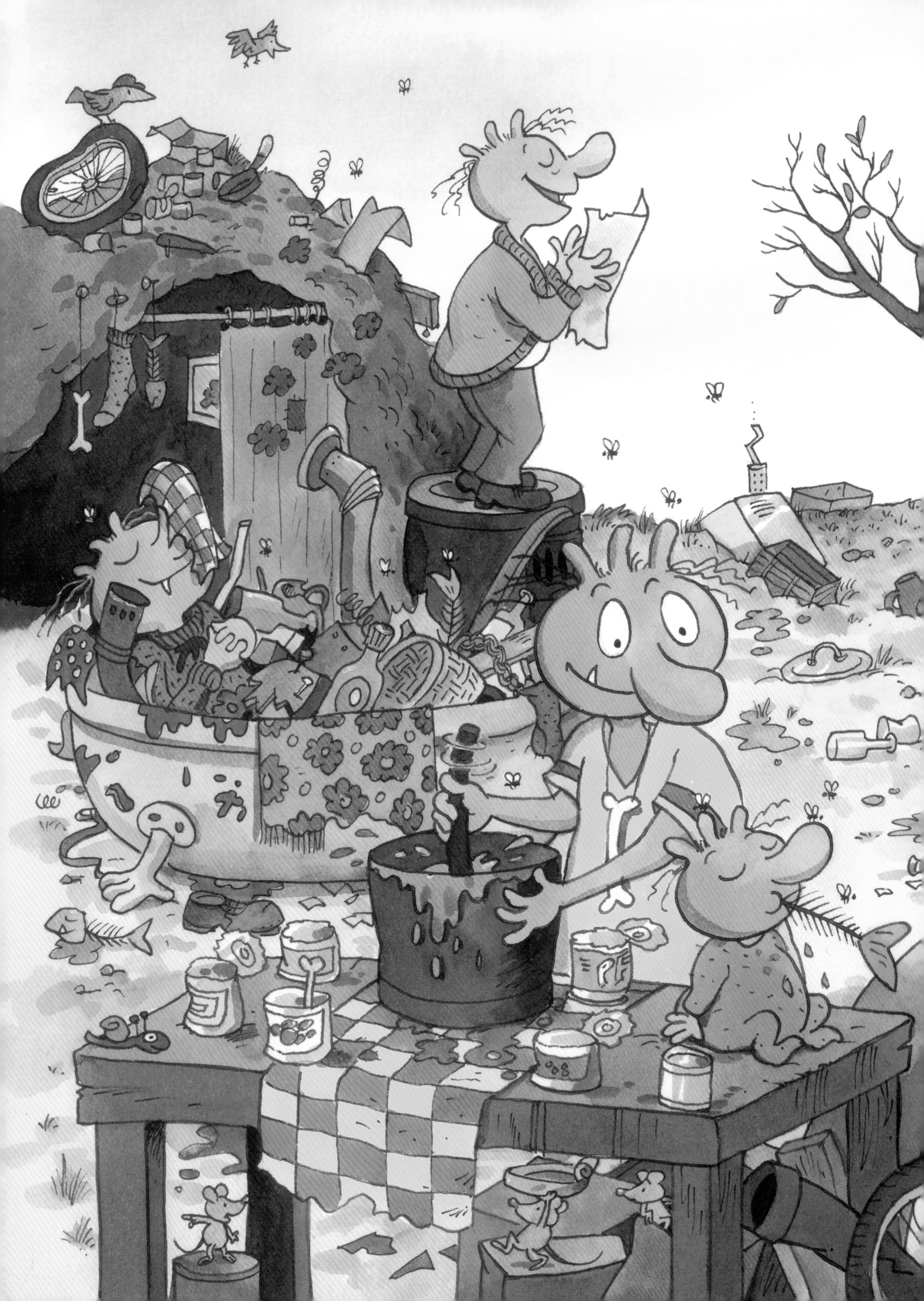

Not long afterward, Oggly-Grandma and the Oggly children are back at the trash dump. Oggly-Mom has cooked a big pot of stinky soup, and Oggly-Baby is gnawing happily at a long fishbone.
Oggly-Dad is still sitting in his trash tub.
Oggly-Grandpa spits something out of his bone pipe onto the ground and clears his throat. He has composed a poem for the Oggly children.

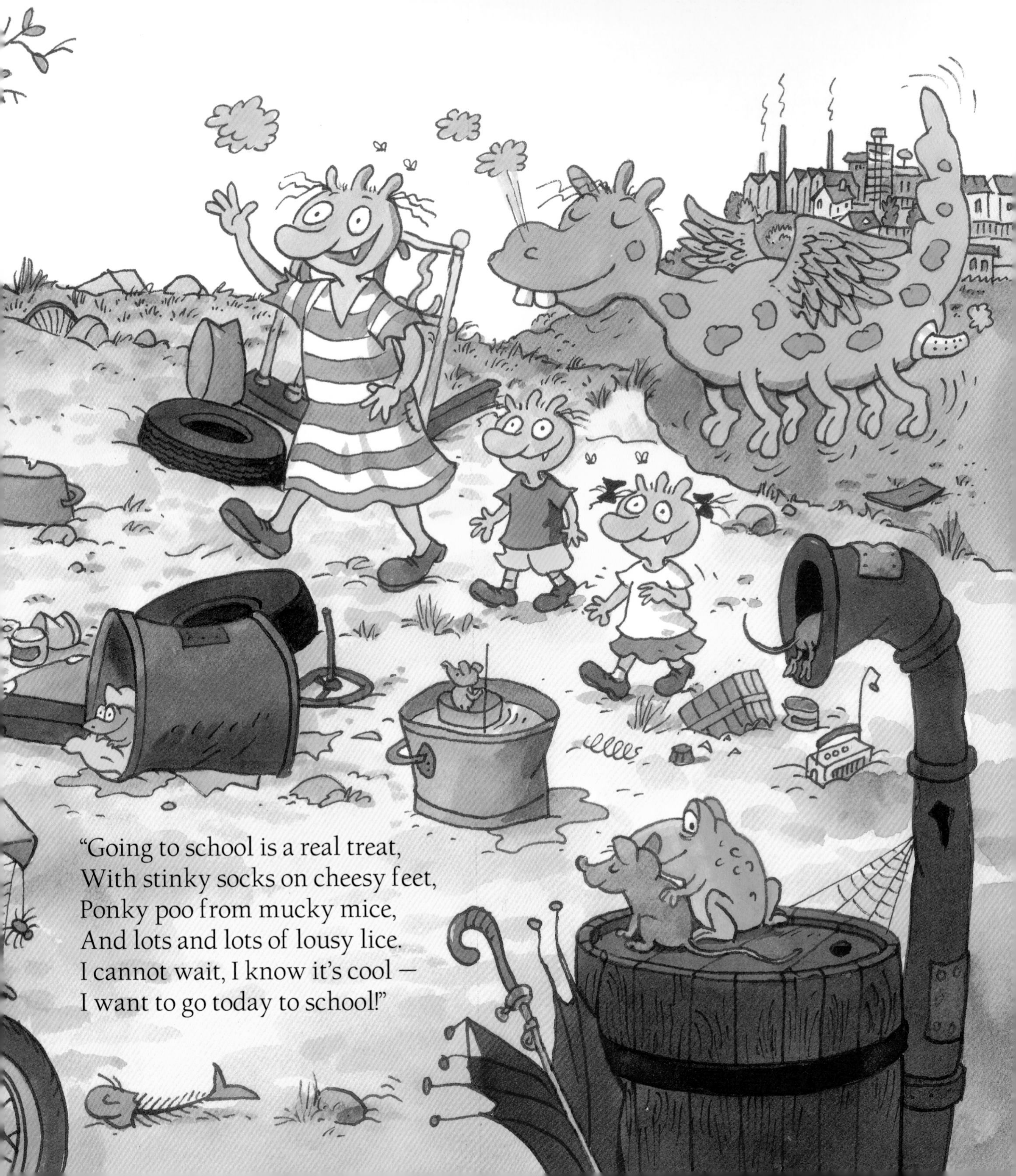

"Going to school is a real treat,
With stinky socks on cheesy feet,
Ponky poo from mucky mice,
And lots and lots of lousy lice.
I cannot wait, I know it's cool –
I want to go today to school!"

"Faboggulous, Grandpa!" cry the Oggly children. "You must come with us to the school tomorrow."
"Us too!" cry Oggly-Mom and Oggly-Dad. "Tomorrow we'll all go together!"

The Mud-Puddle Song

Text by Erhard Deitl
Music by Paloma Ohm

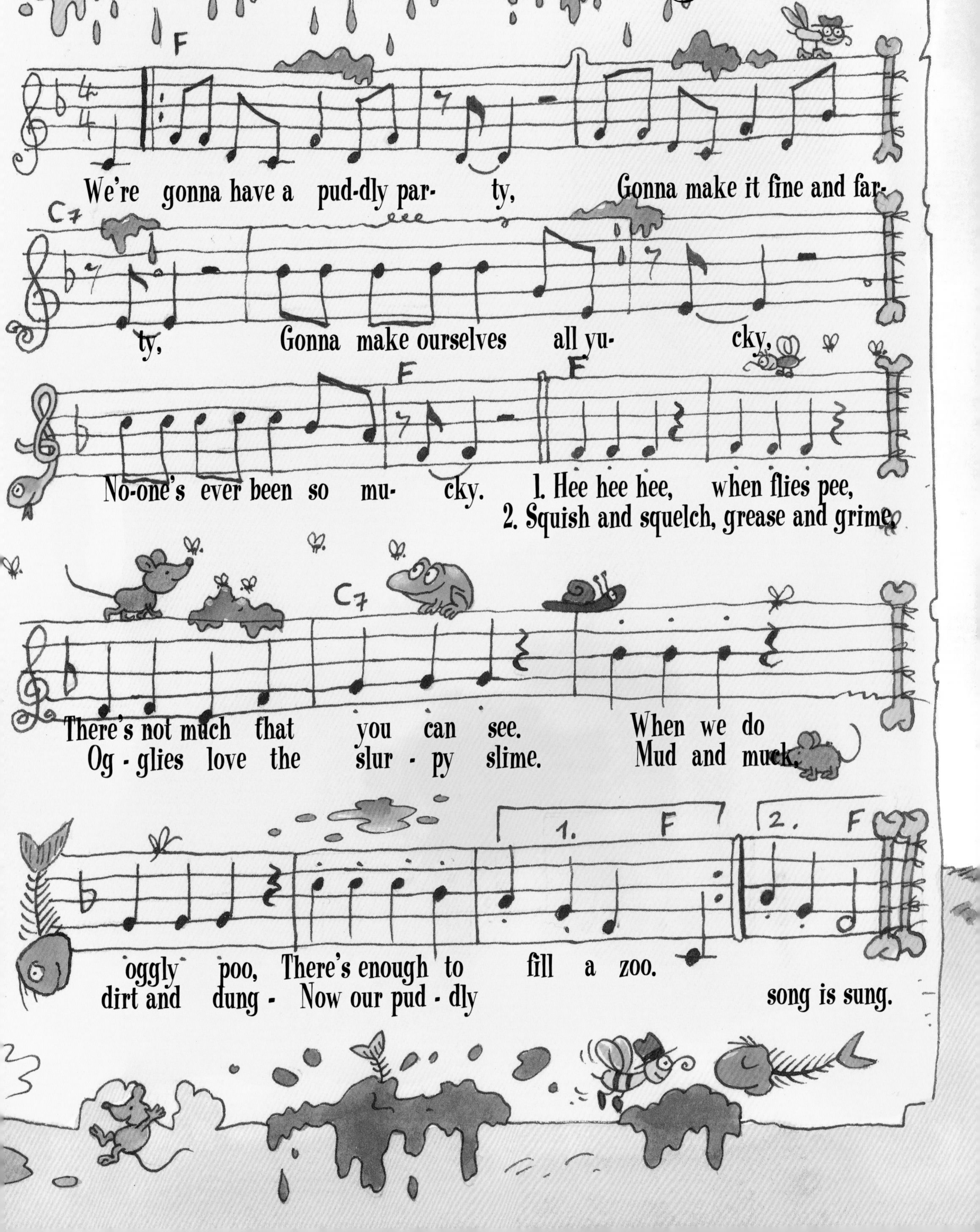
F
We're gonna have a pud-dly par- ty, Gonna make it fine and far-
C7
ty, Gonna make ourselves all yu- cky,
F
No-one's ever been so mu- cky.
F
1. Hee hee hee, when flies pee,
2. Squish and squelch, grease and grime,
C7
There's not much that you can see. When we do
Og - glies love the slur - py slime. Mud and muck,
oggly poo, There's enough to fill a zoo.
dirt and dung - Now our pud - dly song is sung.
1. F
2. F

Ogglies never wash or brush their teeth.

Ogglies hate all the foods we like.

They relish trash, and they love anything rotten or moldy.

They enjoy muck soup with fishbones, shoe-sole schnitzel, and stinky cake.

They love anything with a steamy, stinky stench.

They find the scent of perfume absolutely disgusting.

Ogglies are strong. They can throw a rubber tire sixty feet.

They like to jump around in sludgy puddles of mud.

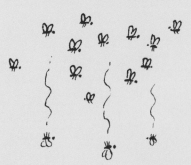

Even flies faint at the reek of their bad breath.

Dragon Firebottom is the Ogglies' pet. They can fly all over the place on his back.